This book is for Z

For information address Hyperion Books for Children,
114 Fifth Avenue, New York, New York 10011-5690.

First Edition

1 3 5 7 9 10 8 6 4 2

Printed in Singapore

Library of Congress Cataloging-in-Publication Data
Raschka, Christopher.
Goosey Goose / by Chris Raschka.—1st ed.
p. cm.— (Thingy things)
Summary: If you mess with Goosey Goose, you will be in trouble.
ISBN 0-7868-0641-9 (trade)
[1. Geese—Fiction.] I. Title.
PZ7.R1814 Go   2000
[E]—dc21   99-51685

Visit www.hyperionchildrensbooks.com

THINGY THINGS
Goosey Goose

Chris Raschka

HYPERION BOOKS FOR CHILDREN
NEW YORK

If you mess with
Goosey Goose,

you are in trouble.
AAAAAWWWWWWWW,
trouble.

Not with her father.

Not with her mother.

Not with her brother.

Not with her sister.

But with her!